Tiptoe Into Scary Cities

SINISTER SAVANNAH

by E. Merwin

Consultant: Debbie Felton
Professor of Classics
University of Massachusetts
Amherst, Massachusetts

BEARPORT PUBLISHING

New York, New York

Credits

Cover, © Sergey Nivens/Shutterstock, © Lisa F. Young/Shutterstock, © popovartem.com/Shutterstock, © f11photo/Shutterstock, © Chuck Wagner/Shutterstock, and © jokerpro/Shutterstock; TOC, © Natalie Bratslavsky/Shutterstock; 4–5, © Sean Pavone/Shutterstock, © Neil Lockhart/Shutterstock, © Everett Historical/Shutterstock, © kanphitchaya/Shutterstock, and © Ewa Studio/Shutterstock; 6, © elwynn/Shutterstock; 7, © William Silver/Shutterstock; 8, © kamnuan/Shutterstock; 8–9, © Alejandro Gherardi/Shutterstock; 10, © PHOTOCREO Michal Bednarek/Shutterstock; 11, © K. L. Howard/Alamy; 12, © Donna Beeler/Shutterstock and © Roman Nerud/Shutterstock; 13, © Gail des Jardin; 14T, © Sarah Marchant/Shutterstock; 14–15, © Rolf_52/Shutterstock; 16, © Jakub Krechowicz/Dreamstime; 17, © Curious Expeditions/CC BY-NC-SA 4.0 and © New York Public Library Digital Collections; 18, © Georgia Historical Society; 19, © Everett-Art/Shutterstock; 20T, © B Isnor/Shutterstock; 20B, © Irina Korsakova/Shutterstock; 21, © meunierd/Shutterstock; 23, © Iryna Liveoak/Shutterstock; 24, © PRILL/Shutterstock.

Publisher: Kenn Goin
Senior Editor: Joyce Tavolacci
Creative Director: Spencer Brinker
Photo Researcher: Thomas Persano
Cover: Kim Jones

Library of Congress Cataloging-in-Publication Data in process at time of publication (2019)
Library of Congress Control Number: 2018009290
ISBN-13: 978-1-68402-667-8 (library binding)

For more information, write to Bearport Publishing Company, Inc., 45 West 21st Street, Suite 3B, New York, New York 10010. Printed in the United States of America.

10 9 8 7 6 5 4 3 2 1

CONTENTS

Sinister Savannah

By day, Savannah, Georgia, is alive. People walk along busy streets. They go in and out of old buildings.

Yet this old city has a spooky past. When the sun sets, it's time for the dead to come to life!

Get ready to read four frightening tales about Savannah. Turn the page . . . if you dare.

A Cold Case

Colonial Park Cemetery

It was a cold winter night in 1901. Samuel T. Baker was walking home. He took a shortcut through Colonial Park **Cemetery.** Without warning, someone hit him hard on the head. Samuel was left to die in a pool of blood. The case was never solved. Someone got away with **murder**!

The entrance to Colonial Park Cemetery

Over 100 years later, a college student visited the cemetery. Suddenly, a man with a bloody skull came into view. He moved toward the student. When she screamed, he **vanished**! Was it Samuel's **spirit**? Was he looking for his killer?

No one knows.

Over 10,000 people are buried in Colonial Park Cemetery.

GIGGLING GHOSTS

Hamilton-Turner Inn

The Hamilton-Turner Inn dates back to 1873. It was once the home of the Hamilton family. It later became an inn filled with **snickering** spirits.

In 1991, a worker at the inn kept hearing children giggling. But there were no kids around. Then she heard a hard ball rolling across the floor. **Puzzled,** she looked to the house's past for answers.

The Hamilton-Turner Inn

The worker learned that the Hamilton family had five children. When the parents threw parties, the children had to stay upstairs. So the kids created their own fun. They rolled pool balls down the staircase. Over 100 years later, their giggling ghosts are still playing the same trick!

Another visitor to the house once heard a ghostly child's voice. It said, "Daddy-Daddy-Daddy-Daddy."

Eat, Drink, and—Be Wary!

The Pirate's House

Built in 1753, the Pirate's House is now a lively restaurant. Long ago, pirates went there to kidnap sailors. The pirates dragged the men into a secret tunnel. The passage led to the Savannah River, where a ship awaited. When the sailors awoke, they were far out to sea!

The Pirate's House restaurant

Today, loud footsteps echo in the dining room. Unexplained moans rise from the tunnel. In the kitchen, an angry ghost glares at the staff. Then it disappears! Have the spirits of the kidnapped sailors returned?

A ghost has also been spotted near the restrooms. He always runs past guests.

Making Waves

Morrell Park

Over 100 years ago, a young Savannah woman made a promise. And, for 44 years, she kept it. Many **witnesses** say she's still keeping it—long after her death.

Florence Martus had a boyfriend who went to sea. She told him she would wait for him.

Florence Martus

Florence promised to wave a white cloth at every ship until he returned. Sadly, the young man never came home.

For 44 years, Florence stood in Morrell Park. By day, she waved the white cloth at every ship she saw. At night, she held up a lantern. She helped over 50,000 ships reach shore!

After her death, a **statue** of Florence was placed in the park. Visitors have seen her ghost there. A shopkeeper says Florence's spirit often whooshes by her. She has also seen a ghostly shadow on the wall of her shop.

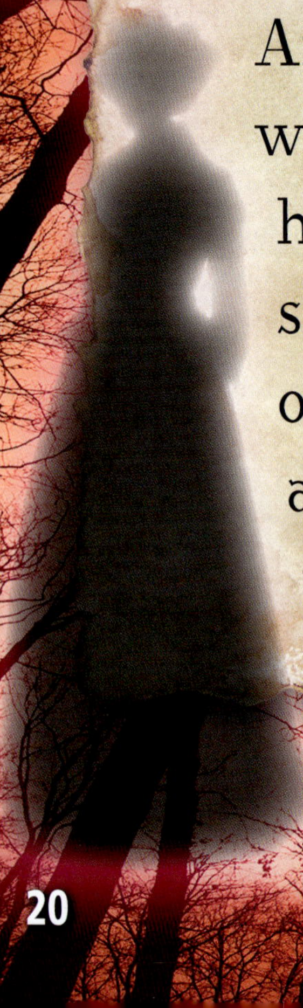

Another shopkeeper says she has seen Florence's spirit, too. It moves around a table where small statues of Florence are sold!

A statue of Florence Martus and her dog in Morrell Park

Spooky Spots in Savannah

GLOSSARY

cemetery (SEM-uh-ter-ee) a place where dead bodies are buried

murder (MUR-der) the killing of another person

puzzled (PUHZ-uhld) confused by something

snickering (SNIK-ur-ing) laughing

spirit (SPIHR-it) an otherworldly being, such as a ghost

statue (STACH-oo) a large stone or metal figure

vanished (VAN-ishd) disappeared completely

witnesses (WIT-niss-ez) people who tell what they saw

Index

Read More

Camisa, Kathryn. *Horror Hotels (Tiptoe Into Scary Places).* New York: Bearport (2017).

Zullo, Allan. *Haunted Kids: True Ghost Stories.* New York: Scholastic (2000).

Learn More Online

To learn more about sinister Savannah, visit:
www.bearportpublishing.com/Tiptoe

About the Author

E. Merwin enjoys researching haunted histories. As for the ghosts, she wishes them well in this world—and the next.